MW00610053

The Little Girl

小女孩

The Little Girl

小女孩

By Phil Wong

Paintings by Fenlin Lee

New Earth Enterprises

The Little Girl
Text Copyright © 2008 by Philip M. Wong
Illustrations Copyright © 2008 by Fenlin Lee

Designed by Joy Versluys

Published by New Earth Enterprises, Saline, Michigan, USA
Visit us on the web at www.adoption-by-grace.com.
For a pronunciation key of Chinese names, visit www.adoption-by-grace.com/pronunciation.html.

All rights reserved. No part of this book may be reproduced or transmitted in any form by any means, electronic or mechanical, including photocopying and recording, or by any information storage and retrieval system.

Printed in USA

To all the little girls of the world.
Your Defender never slumbers. PMW

*O*nce there was a little girl who had a dream. She dreamed that there were two strong arms underneath her, holding her tightly. She felt the rhythmic breathing of the person who held her. She saw the smiling face. She heard the deep hum of a song. And the last thing she remembered in her dream was the kiss on her forehead.

But when she woke from her dream, she felt a cold spring breeze. She was very hungry and started to cry.

A man on his bicycle heard the sound of crying. He went over and saw the little girl in a basket. He looked around and called out, "Hello! Hello!" But no one answered.

The man started talking to himself.

"I can't take care of a little girl! I must get to work."

"What if you were that little baby? Wouldn't you want somebody to help you?"

"It's not my responsibility! It would be different if I had a wife. Think of all the trouble a baby would cause for me!"

"She's so little and helpless."

Just then the little girl filled her lungs with air and cried even louder.

"Well, let's see if I can warm her up," the man said to himself, "and then let's find out where she belongs."

So he skillfully tied the basket to the back of his bicycle, turned around and rode back home.

The man wrapped the little girl in a shirt. He was greatly relieved when she finally stopped crying. But in a few minutes the crying started again.

"Ai yaa!" he said aloud. It was mid-morning and he had not yet started work! So he put the little girl on the back of his bike and rode off.

When he returned home that evening, he said to the little girl, "I am never going to find your parents, am I? What shall I call you? Since you will be my bright pearl, I shall call you Ming Zhu.

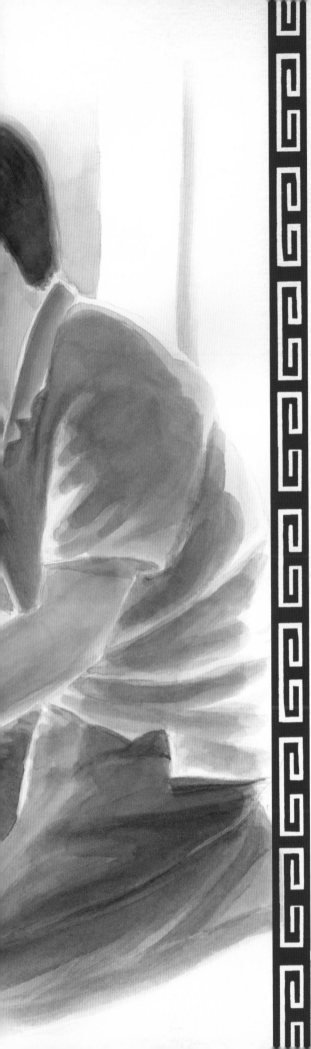

*I*n the course of time, Ming Zhu grew. One evening, Ming Zhu was holding on to a chair. The man, whose name was Li Feng, knelt on the floor and held out his arms. He smiled and said, "Come to Papa." She took a few steps toward Li Feng and started to fall. But he quickly caught her in his hands.

Li Feng was a carpenter. Ming Zhu often watched him as he worked. She noticed that he had very strong hands, hands that were rough from long days of work.

One day as Ming Zhu watched her Papa, she heard a bird chirping nearby. As she listened, she made up a little song. Li Feng heard the song and paused from his work to turn his head and to watch. He smiled.

Ming Zhu watched Li Feng look down the edge of a twisted board. And somehow her Papa managed to make that board straight and true. When he was finished, Ming Zhu ran her hand over the smooth tabletop. "This is a nice table, Papa," she said.

"Thank you, Ming Zhu," Li Feng replied.

One night at dinner, Ming Zhu watched her Papa scoop rice into his mouth with his chopsticks. She ran over to the drawer and found a pair for herself. She started to scoop from her bowl and spilled half of the rice on her lap.

"Ming Zhu!" Li Feng said in a sharp voice.

Ming Zhu gave a little jump in her chair. Then her eyes filled with tears and she started to cry.

"There, there, Ming Zhu. Don't cry. Everything is all right," said Li Feng. "Do you know what I'm going to do? I'm going to cook something special for you. Do you want to be my helper?"

The next day was Sunday. They woke early and went to the market. Ming Zhu rode on a little bicycle seat made by Li Feng.

"What are you going to cook, Papa?" asked Ming Zhu.

"Sticky rice wrapped in bamboo leaves," Li Feng replied. "My mother used to make these. I learned from her. I'll show you when we get home."

Father and daughter spent much of the day chopping mushrooms, cooking the rice and the pork, carefully wrapping the mixture in the bamboo leaves and tying it all up with string. Then, into the steamer.

Li Feng unwrapped one of the little packages into

Ming Zhu's bowl.

"Well, how do you like it?"

"It's delicious! May I please have another?"

After they had cleaned up, Ming Zhu got ready for bed. "Tell me a story, Papa! Please?" Li Feng told Ming Zhu the story of Dragon and Rat.

"One more story, please, Papa! Please! Just one more?"

No one but Ming Zhu had taken such an interest in his story telling. So, late into the night, Li Feng told her the story of Fa Mu Lan, the famous woman warrior.

Ming Zhu's eyes finally grew heavy. The carpenter kissed her on the forehead and said goodnight.

One day Ming Zhu was riding with her Papa on their bike. She tried to reach the pedals but started to bump Li Feng's legs as he pedaled along.

Later that day, when Li Feng was in his workshop, Ming Zhu found a chair and dragged it over to the bike. She managed to get into her seat. The bicycle rolled down a little hill. At first it was great fun, but then she started going faster and faster. Ming Zhu fell and let out a cry.

Li Feng recognized her voice and came running. He picked Ming Zhu up in his arms, carried her back home, washed and bandaged her and put her to bed. Li Feng looked at her and saw a very sad Ming Zhu who said that she would never ride a bicycle without her Papa ever again.

"Do you know how to play cloth, rock, scissors?" Li
Feng asked.

"No," replied Ming Zhu.

"Would you like me to teach you?" asked Li Feng.

"Playing with rocks and scissors sounds too dangerous, Papa," said Ming Zhu.

"No, no. It's not dangerous. Look, this is cloth," he said as he held out a flat hand.

"This is rock," he said making a fist.

"And these are scissors," he said as he made his two fingers move up and down. "Cloth covers rock. Scissors cut cloth and rock breaks scissors."

"We both count to three and then you pick cloth, rock or scissors and I do the same. Ready? One. Two. Three. Go!"

Ming Zhu chose rock. Li Feng chose scissors. "Oh, you got me," he said.

"Ready? One. Two. Three. Go!"

Ming Zhu chose cloth. Li Feng, who had a quick eye and was watching Ming Zhu very carefully, chose rock.

"Oh, you got me again!"

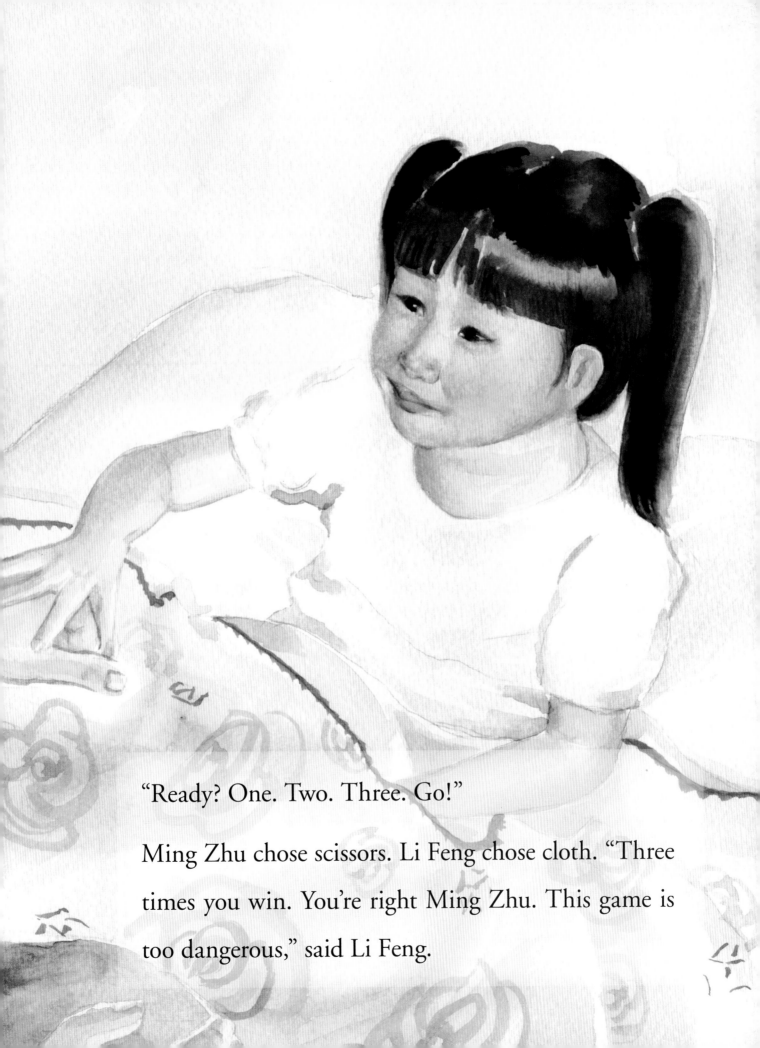

"Ready? One. Two. Three. Go!"

Ming Zhu chose scissors. Li Feng chose cloth. "Three times you win. You're right Ming Zhu. This game is too dangerous," said Li Feng.

"Papa," Ming Zhu scolded, "You let me win!" Her eyebrows went into a deep frown. Li Feng's eyebrows went into a deep frown. Finally, Ming Zhu couldn't keep her eyebrows down any more. They laughed together.

By the time Ming Zhu was eleven, she had long outgrown the little seat made by Li Feng. She had ridden on the rack above the rear wheel for quite some time. On her twelfth birthday, Li Feng gave Ming Zhu a bicycle of her very own. Ming Zhu's mind flashed back to that frightful day long ago when she fell from her Papa's bicycle. But not wanting to hurt her Papa's feelings, she smiled and thanked him for the wonderful new bicycle.

"Would you like to try it out?" asked Li Feng.

And in a few moments, Ming Zhu overcame her fear of riding a bicycle without her Papa. She settled into the seat and started to pedal.

That night, Ming Zhu grew sick. Her face was hot and red and her throat burned. She started to cry. Li Feng woke up and came over to her bed. He gave her a drink of water and put a cold cloth on her forehead. Ming Zhu started to cough. It was a terrible cough, the kind that makes your sides hurt. All night Li Feng sat by her bed and held her hand. His eyes and mind grew weary. His back ached. Just as he dozed off, the rooster crowed.

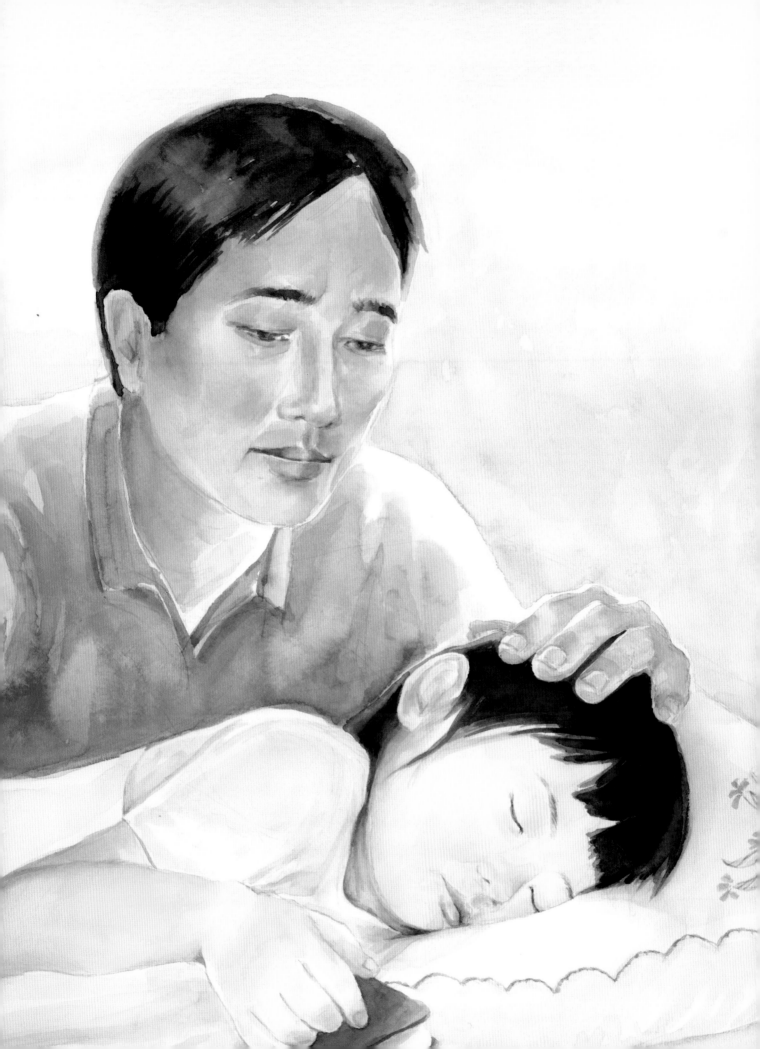

For her eighteenth birthday, Li Feng gave Ming Zhu a chi pao. Her face shone with a serene glow as she stroked the soft fabric. Ming Zhu tried it on and when Li Feng saw his daughter in her new dress with her hair down to her waist, a strange feeling came over him, a feeling that something was not quite right. He shook the feeling out of his heart and smiled over his daughter. But his smile faded and the feeling crept back.

"Put your dress away now, my dear little girl. It's Sunday and we're having a guest, my old classmate, Chen Zu Kang. So we have to go to the market."

They rode their bicycles together and bought all the ingredients for tofu soup and steamed fish in black bean sauce. Chen Zu Kang arrived and greeted Li Feng.

"Hello my friend. It's been a long time. You look good," said Chen Zu Kang.

"Good to see you again. Please come in. Sit down and have some tea," said Li Feng.

"And who is this?" asked Chen Zu Kang.

"This is my daughter, Ming Zhu," replied Li Feng.

"Nice to meet you, Mr. Chen," said Ming Zhu.

"Nice to meet you," said Chen Zu Kang as he placed his carved walking stick next to the door.

Over their meal, Li Feng and Chen Zu Kang talked. Chen Zu Kang noticed how cheerfully Ming Zhu refilled his soup bowl.

Chen Zu Kang said, "Tell me, Ming Zhu, what are your days like?"

"I help my Papa in his workshop. We go to the market together. I manage the household. And when I have time, I love to read," replied Ming Zhu.

"What have you been reading?" asked Chen Zu Kang.

"I'm reading an epic about a hero who came down from heaven to save the world from its darkest danger."

As Ming Zhu washed the dishes in the kitchen, Chen Zu Kang said in a low voice, "Li Feng, I would like to introduce my nephew to your daughter. His name is Gao Xin."

"Perhaps," said Li Feng. "Tell me about this nephew."

The next Sunday, Li Feng and Ming Zhu rode to the market to buy the ingredients for steamed pork buns and bok choy with mushrooms.

"We're having guests today. Chen Zu Kang and his nephew," said Li Feng.

After their guests had dined and departed, Li Feng asked Ming Zhu, "What did you think of Mr. Gao?"

"He seems like a good nephew. I saw him help his uncle up the step," replied Ming Zhu.

"Gao Xin would like you to be his wife, Ming Zhu," said Li Feng.

Ming Zhu stared for a moment. Li Feng knew she was going to cry by the way her lips crumpled.

"But, Papa, I don't want to be his wife. I want to stay home with you!" cried Ming Zhu as she buried her face in her Papa's chest.

"There, there, my dear girl. Don't cry. Ming Zhu, your Papa grows old. I feel it in my bones. I can't make a table as quickly as I did when I was a young man. I won't be able to take care of you forever. Gao Xin is a good man. He's a hard worker. He will treat you well. And you can come and visit me. But it's for you to decide. You may stay home with me if you like."

So in the course of time, the restaurant brought out the red tablecloths. Behind the main table they hung "double happiness." Ming Zhu was dressed in her chi pao. Gao Xin wore a grey shirt and matching pants. Chen Zu Kang and Gao Xin's parents were there along with the other guests. Throughout the meal, Li Feng thought back to all the happy times he had shared with Ming Zhu. "It's time for her to go," he said to himself. "She's a young woman now. She looks happy. And so does Gao Xin."

The next day, Li Feng made rice porridge for breakfast. He went to the workshop and started to choose some boards for a new table. He felt a terrible loneliness. He had often been alone before finding Ming Zhu, but this was the first time he noticed that he was alone. He sat down, stared at the boards and started talking to himself.

"I don't feel

like making a table today."

"Hmmm. And why is that, Li Feng?"

"Mind your own business, will you?"

"Well, if you aren't going to make a table,

what will you do?"

"I think I'll stare at these boards some more."

"And how long will you do that?"

"Why do you keep asking me all these questions?"

"Do you know what will happen if you

stare at those boards long enough?"

"Leave me alone."

"You'll starve."

No reply.

"Didn't your father ever tell you that if a man will

not work, he shall not eat?"

"All right! All right! I'll make the table."

*I*n the course of time, Ming Zhu became great with child. She gave birth to a little girl. One Sunday, after Ming Zhu had a long rest, she wrapped the baby up with many, many blankets. The only way you could tell it was a baby was by looking into the tiny face that peered through the great bundle. "Time for your first bicycle ride," said Ming Zhu.

Gao Xin pedaled. Ming Zhu rode on the rack above the rear wheel, holding the baby tightly.

Li Feng was in his workshop when he heard Ming Zhu call, "Papa! Papa!" He wiped the sawdust from his hands and went out to meet her.

"Meet your granddaughter, Papa," said Ming Zhu.

"She looks just like you did when you were a baby, Ming Zhu," said Li Feng. "And what is her name?"

"You choose, Papa," answered Ming Zhu.

"Me?" asked Li Feng. He looked at Gao Xin.

"You choose, Papa," said Gao Xin.

"Hmm. What shall I call you? You are my little treasure so I shall name you Jia Zhen."

That night, Ming Zhu had a dream. She dreamed that there were two strong arms underneath her, holding her tightly. She felt the rhythmic breathing of the person who held her. She saw the smiling face. She heard the deep hum of a song. And the last thing she remembered in her dream was the kiss on her forehead.

*S*o over the course of time, Ming Zhu and her family often visited Li Feng and they were all very happy together. Li Feng watched his granddaughter grow until he was old and full of years.

Afterword

"Zhang shang ming zhu" is a Chinese idiom that means "bright pearl in the palm of the hand." From this expression, Ming Zhu has become a name for an only daughter, especially in rural China. Our bright pearl, Ming Zhu, represents all the precious girls of China and the world. May *The Little Girl* turn the hearts of fathers and mothers to their daughters. To find out more, please visit us at www.adoption-by-grace.com.

Acknowledgments

I am grateful to my dear wife, Kristin, for carefully editing the text and for her persevering encouragement; to Fenlin Lee for her brilliant watercolors; to Joy Versluys for expertly designing the book; to Ching Ru Wang for providing the Chinese characters; to Janet Chen for her myriad contributions; to David and Margaret Baker and Steve Landrum for all their wise counsel; and to all those who advocated for *The Little Girl*.

PMW

Many thanks to Mom, Dad, Fulin, Janet Chen, Pastor Randy and Dawn Cutter, friends at New Dawn and friends at work for their encouragement for my art; and to Phil and Kristin for their kindness and heart for children.

Special blessings to all mothers and fathers who adopt and may every baby know their parents' love.

FL

About the Author

Phil Wong was born in Boston, Massachusetts. He attended the University of Michigan and the University of California, San Diego. Phil is married to Kristin and has two daughters by birth, Kathryn and Clara, and two adopted sons from Vietnam, Benjamin and Josiah. Living in China for a year and his experiences in Vietnam were Phil's inspiration for *The Little Girl*.

Phil and Kristin enjoy reading books with their children and having friends over for dinner. The Wongs worship at Knox Presbyterian Church in Ann Arbor, Michigan.

About the Artist

Fenlin Lee was born in Taiwan. Her first grade teacher saw Fenlin's drawing of a bird and became the first to recognize her gift for art. Fenlin went on to graduate from the Pratt Institute in New York with her Bachelor of Arts in Visual Communications Design.

Fenlin enjoys using color and design and finds inspiration from music, dance and the visual aspects of different cultures. But her biggest inspiration is Jesus. "I feel the pictures I see are a gift from him and I like to use my art to encourage people and to honor God, even if it is a small, simple picture."

Fenlin lives in Fort Lauderdale, Florida.

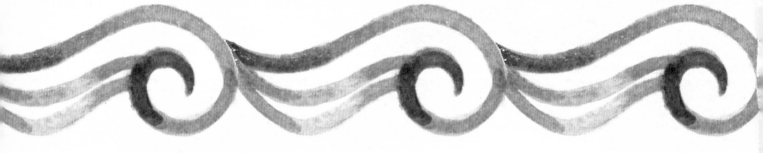